The Printer

*In loving memory of Louis Uhlberg, the Printer,
and his wife, Sarah, my beautiful mother.*

—M.U.

ACKNOWLEDGMENT

To recreate the setting of this story, the pressroom of *The New York Daily News* in 1940, I was fortunate to have the cooperation of Sean Cox, who is known as that paper's "institutional memory." I owe him thanks for his endless patience in taking me through the intricate process of creating, on a daily basis, over two million copies of what was at that time the most widely read newspaper in America. But more importantly, Sean's detailed descriptions of that long gone pressroom brought a memory vividly back to mind. Once again, I could see standing in that enormous room, my father, *The Printer*.

Ω

Published by
PEACHTREE PUBLISHERS
1700 Chattahoochee Avenue
Atlanta, Georgia 30318-2112

www.peachtree-online.com

Text ©2003 by Myron Uhlberg
Illustrations©2003 by Henri Sørensen

Book design by Loraine M. Joyner

Manufactured in Singapore

10 9 8 7 6 5 4 3 2

ISBN 1-56145-221-1

Library of Congress Cataloging-in-Publication Data

Uhlberg, Myron.
  The printer / written by Myron Uhlberg ; illustrated by Henri Sorensen.
     p. cm.
Summary: A boy recalls the day his deaf father saved everyone's life when fire broke out at the newspaper printing plant where he worked.
  ISBN 1-56145-221-1
  [1. Fathers--Fiction. 2. Deaf--Fiction. 3. People with disabilities--Fiction. 4. Sign language--Fiction. 5. Newspaper buildings--Fiction.] I. Sorensen, Henri, ill. II. Title.
  PZ7.U3257 Pr 2003
  [Fic]--dc21   2003001600

Myron Uhlberg

Illustrated by
Henri Sørensen

The Printer

PEACHTREE
ATLANTA

y father was a printer. He wore a printer's four-cornered newspaper hat. Every day after work, he brought home the next day's paper. After reading it, he always folded a page into a small hat and gently placed it on my head.

I would not take off my newspaper hat until bedtime.

My father was deaf. Though he could not hear, he felt through the soles of his shoes the pounding and rumbling of the giant printing presses that daily spat out the newspaper he helped create.

As a boy, my father learned how to speak with his hands. As a man, he learned how to turn lead-type letters into words and sentences. My father loved being a printer.

Sometimes my father felt sad about the way he was treated by his fellow workers who could hear. Because they couldn't talk to him with their hands, they seemed to ignore him. Years went by as my father and the hearing printers worked side by side. They never once exchanged a single thought.

But my father did not lack friends. There were other printers at the plant who were deaf. They had also learned to talk with their hands.

ne day, while the giant presses ran, their noises shutting out all other sound, my father spotted a fire flickering in a far corner of the pressroom.

The fire was spreading quickly, silently. Suddenly, the wood floor burst into flames.

My father knew he had to tell everyone. He couldn't speak to shout a warning. Even if he could, no one would hear him over the loud roar of the presses.

But he could speak with his hands.

He did not hesitate. He jumped onto an ink drum and waved his arms excitedly until, clear across the room, he caught the attention of a fellow printer who also couldn't hear a sound.

My father's hands shouted through the terrible noise of the printing presses,

FIRE! FIRE!
TELL EVERYONE TO GET OUT!
TELL THE HEARING ONES!

His friend climbed onto a huge roll of newsprint. His fingers screamed to the other deaf workers,

FIRE! FIRE!
TELL THE HEARING ONES!

All the printers who couldn't hear ran to fellow workers who could. They pointed to the fire, which had now spread to the wall next to the only exit.

Not one of my father's friends left until everyone
knew of the danger. My father was the last to escape.

By the time everyone had fled, the fire—feeding on huge quantities of paper—had engulfed the enormous plant. The giant presses, some still spewing out burning sheets of newspaper, had fallen partly through the floor. Great shafts of flame shot out of the bursting windows.

The printers stood in the street, broken glass at their feet. They embraced one another as the fire engines arrived. They were happy to be alive.

My father stood alone, struck numb by the last image of the burning presses.

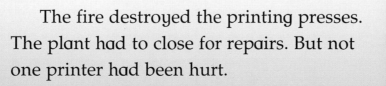

The fire destroyed the printing presses. The plant had to close for repairs. But not one printer had been hurt.

hen the printing plant finally reopened, my father went back to the work he loved. The new presses were switched on and roared into life.

When the day's newspaper had been printed, the presses shuddered to a stop. Now there was silence.

In the midst of the stillness, my father's co-workers gathered around him. They presented him with a hat made of the freshly printed newspaper.

And as my father put the hat on his head, all the printers who could hear did something surprising.

They told him THANK YOU with their hands.

That night, my father picked up the newspaper hat that his fellow printers had given him. After adjusting the four corners, he placed it gently on my head. I didn't take off my hat, but wore it carefully to bed.

I imagined I was standing next to my father on a vast printing press floor, turning lead-type letters into words and sentences. We were wearing four-cornered newspaper hats.

We were printers.

Author's Note

HIS STORY IS A WORK OF FICTION. Parts of it, however, are based in truth.

MY FATHER WAS A PRINTER. He worked in the composing room of *The New York Daily News* for over forty years. It was the only job he ever had, and he loved it. In the mid-1940s, which is the time setting for this story, newspapers were the key source of daily news for Americans. Television, computers, and the internet as we know them today were yet to be invented. Newspapers were read by 85 percent of the American people. My father was understandably proud of his daily contribution—composing a single page of a great metropolitan newspaper that would be reproduced on giant printing presses two million times a day.

MY FATHER WAS DEAF. His parents and siblings could hear. Because he could not fully communicate with them, he often felt lonely, even though they loved him dearly. But he had no words to express how he felt. While my father was still a young boy, his parents sent him to live in a deaf school. There he learned sign language, the language of the deaf. Every hour of every day, he eagerly learned new words. Now he could listen to others and tell how he felt, how he thought, and finally, how he imagined he would live in a hearing world.

In the early 1900s, when my father was a young boy, many hearing people thought that the deaf could not learn as well as the hearing. In those days, deaf children were usually taught how to work with their hands.

MY FATHER AND MANY OTHERS were taught to be printers. This was viewed as the ideal trade for the deaf since printing was a very noisy business. My father worked in the composing room. He assembled hot metal lines of type, called slugs, which were created on a loud, clattering Linotype machine. This was a heavy iron device with a keyboard similar to a typewriter. My father arranged the slugs, along with loose metal type, into a metal frame. The metal frame was then used to create a printing plate that would eventually be attached to a printing press, another noisy machine that was as large as a small house.

WHEN I WAS A SMALL BOY, my father took me to the place where he worked. *The New York Daily News* building appeared to me like a concrete mountain. No matter how far back I tilted my head, I could never see where it ended. When my father took me around the pressroom, I had to put the ends of my fingers in my ears to muffle the noise. When the presses were rolling, they were as loud as a herd of thundering elephants!

PRINTERS DID WEAR the four-cornered newspaper hats in the 1940s, and they still wear them today. The hat protects the printer's hair from the fine particles of ink that the high-speed presses spray into the air. My father often made hats for me when I was a boy, to my great delight.

–M. U.
2003

My father and I communicated with each other using American Sign Language, or ASL for short. It was the first language I learned as a child. ASL uses precise hand positions along with facial expressions, as well as movement of the arms, shoulders, and even the entire body.

The word "fire" is used several times in this story. It is signed by wiggling the five fingers of each hand while the hands move up and down. This movement suggests the many tongues of flame leaping from the heart of a fire.

In ASL, just as in English, fire can be better described by the use of adjectives, such as big or great. In this story, the printer wiggled his ten fingers vigorously while raising and lowering his hands steeply and rapidly to signal the intensity of the fire in the printing pressroom. The expression on the printer's face also helped convey a sense of urgency to the others.

For links to interesting sources on this topic, visit the Peachtree Publishers website at peachtree-online.com.

Why a newspaper hat?

With printing presses running at speeds up to 20 miles per hour and 70,000 newspapers being printed, trimmed, folded, and bound into bundles every hour, a fine mist of paper dust and ink is thrown into the air. Pressmen often fashion a paper hat like the one shown here to keep the ink and dust out of their hair.

NEWSPAPER PRINTER'S HAT

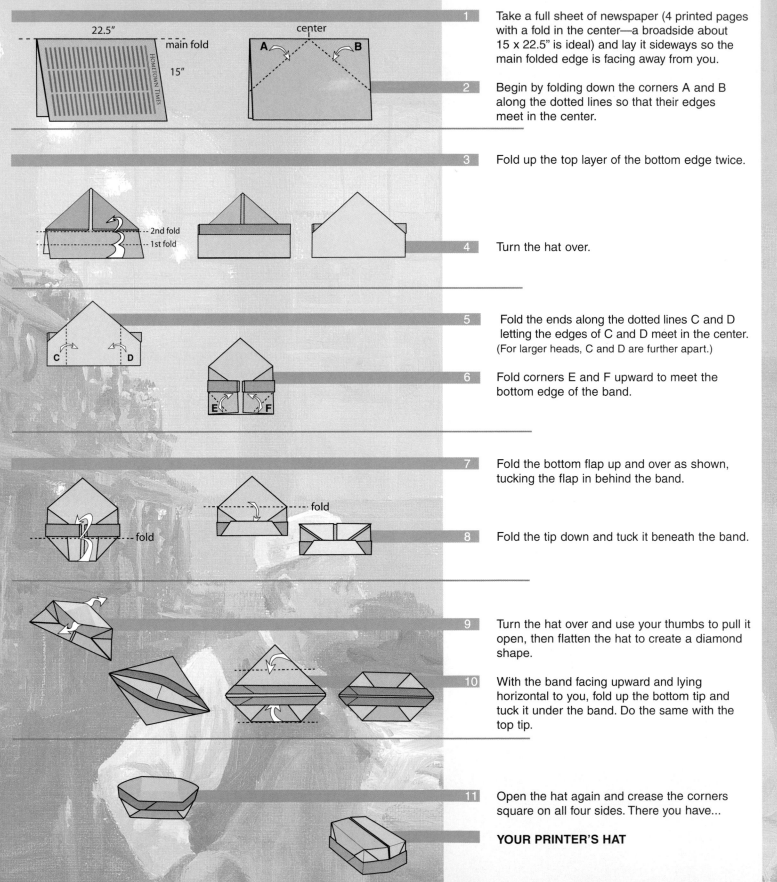

1. Take a full sheet of newspaper (4 printed pages with a fold in the center—a broadside about 15 x 22.5" is ideal) and lay it sideways so the main folded edge is facing away from you.

2. Begin by folding down the corners A and B along the dotted lines so that their edges meet in the center.

3. Fold up the top layer of the bottom edge twice.

4. Turn the hat over.

5. Fold the ends along the dotted lines C and D letting the edges of C and D meet in the center. (For larger heads, C and D are further apart.)

6. Fold corners E and F upward to meet the bottom edge of the band.

7. Fold the bottom flap up and over as shown, tucking the flap in behind the band.

8. Fold the tip down and tuck it beneath the band.

9. Turn the hat over and use your thumbs to pull it open, then flatten the hat to create a diamond shape.

10. With the band facing upward and lying horizontal to you, fold up the bottom tip and tuck it under the band. Do the same with the top tip.

11. Open the hat again and crease the corners square on all four sides. There you have...

YOUR PRINTER'S HAT